W9-AFN-831

Stranded

"The bus stops just around the corner," Patti told us.

We waited across from a park. Kids were flying kites, there was a man selling balloons, and a crowd had gathered to watch a juggler.

"Here's the bus," Patti announced. She walked up the steps, expecting us to follow her on.

"Look, Kate, it's the mime we saw on Friday night!" I exclaimed, running around the back of the bus to see better. Kate was right behind me . . .

. . . and the bus and Patti left without us!

Look for these and other books
in the Sleepover Friends Series:

Lauren's Big Mix-Up

Susan Saunders

AN
APPLE
PAPERBACK

SCHOLASTIC INC.
New York Toronto London Auckland Sydney

No part of this publication may be reproduced in whole or in part, or stored in a retrieval system, or transmitted in any form or by any means, electronic, mechanical, photocopying, recording, or otherwise, without written permission of the publisher. For information regarding permission, write to Scholastic Inc., 730 Broadway, New York, NY 10003.

ISBN 0-590-41336-8

Copyright © 1988 by Daniel Weiss Associates, Inc. All rights reserved. Published by Scholastic Inc. APPLE PAPERBACKS is a registered trademark of Scholastic Inc.

12 11 10 9 8 7 6 5 4 3 2   8 9/8 0 1 2 3/9

Printed in the U.S.A.   28

First Scholastic printing, April 1988

Chapter
1

The bus rolled out of the tunnel and started up the curving ramp to the station. For a minute or two we could see the bright lights of the city spread out in front of us.

"There's the Hanover Tower — the one with the red, white, and blue spotlights," Stephanie Green pointed out. "It's the tallest building in town."

"We know that, Stephanie. It's not as though we've never been to the city before," Kate Beekman said huffily. "Didn't our whole class go to the museum in October?"

"It looks a little different at night, that's all," said Stephanie.

"Right — scarier," Patti Jenkins murmured.

It was kind of overwhelming — cars, trucks, and buses racing up the long, straight avenues, horns honking, a fire engine tearing around a corner with its siren screaming, the sidewalks busy with people.

"It's not exactly the three dumb country mice visiting the smart city mouse!" Kate was still grumbling, so I gave her a poke with my elbow — I'm Lauren Hunter. I didn't want to spend the whole city sleepover listening to Kate and Stephanie argue about what was better: the city, or Riverhurst, where all four of us live now.

But Stephanie wasn't paying any attention. She was staring out the back window of the bus at the twinkling skyline. "There's the Barrymore Theater," she said excitedly. "Right next to it is Scrumptious, the restaurant where I had my surprise seventh-birthday party — it has these enormous ice-cream desserts. And a skating rink's on the very top of that round building — you can look out over the whole city while you skate. Two streets over are all the best stores."

Stephanie had lived in the city until the summer before fourth grade, when her family moved to a house on Pine Street in Riverhurst, just down from Kate and me. Stephanie and I got to be friends because we were both in Mr. Civello's fourth-grade class. I liked hearing about the city, and what Stephanie had done there, and the famous people she'd seen.

2

Kate didn't like it nearly as well as I did. Kate and I have been friends forever. We live just one house apart, and we've spent more time together than with anybody else, except maybe our parents. When we were little, we'd play together every day, and in kindergarten we started sleeping at each other's house every Friday. The Sleepover Twins, Kate's dad named us. We'd dress up in our mothers' clothes and play grown-ups, and "let's pretend."

In the early days, we ate hundreds of platters of peanut butter and marshmallow fluff graham crackers, Kool Pops, and Twinkies. As we got older we graduated to my special invention — onion-soup-olives-bacon-bits-and-sour-cream dip, Kate's super fudge, bushels of barbecue potato chips, and gallons of Dr. Pepper. We watched all the old movies on TV, because Kate's interested in making her own movies some day, and played Truth or Dare and Mad Libs.

It had always been just the two of us, so I think Kate felt kind of funny when I asked Stephanie to one of our Friday sleepovers. Next Stephanie invited us to spend the night at her house — she has her own TV set — and Mrs. Green made great peanut-butter chocolate-chip cookies. Then the three of us started hanging around together, but that doesn't mean there weren't problems. Sometimes Kate thought

Stephanie was showing off, and Stephanie thought Kate was being bossy, and I'd be caught in the middle. I was really glad when Patti Jenkins turned up in our fifth-grade class this year to kind of even things out.

Kate was wrong when she called Stephanie the city mouse and the rest of us country mice, because Patti has lived in the city, too. In fact, she and Stephanie even went to the same school for a couple of years, although I never think of Patti doing city things. Stephanie loves excitement, which is why she likes the city so much, but Patti's shy, and she feels a lot more comfortable in Riverhurst. "It's calmer, and quieter — and prettier," she said right away. Kate and I both liked Patti from the start, and before long there were four Sleepover Friends.

As the bus pulled into its parking space at the station, I said, "This'll be fun — and it'll give us something interesting to put in our journals."

Our teacher, Mrs. Mead, had asked the class to keep journals for a month. She wasn't going to read them, she said — that wasn't the point — so we could record anything we felt like writing. Mrs. Mead just wanted us to get in the habit of writing every day. So the four of us went to Riverhurst Stationery and bought four notebooks, exactly alike.

My journal had already begun to repeat itself:

"Tuesday. The weather was warm. Stephanie, Kate, Patti, and I rode to school together on our bikes. We had a math test. I think I got everything right. Jenny Carlin" — she's a girl in our class who I can't stand — "was batting her eyes at Pete and Michael and some of the other boys in the cafeteria at lunch.

"Wednesday. Stephanie, Kate, Patti, and I rode to school together."

Now at least I could write: "Friday. At six o'clock, Stephanie, Kate, Patti, and I took the bus by ourselves into the city."

"There's Nana!" Stephanie exclaimed. She tapped on the window and waved to a small, gray-haired woman in a dark red coat. The woman smiled and waved back. "Nana" is what Stephanie calls her grandmother, Mrs. Bricker. The four of us were spending the weekend at her apartment.

"Welcome!" Mrs. Bricker said as we piled off the bus. "It's so nice to see you all."

Stephanie gave her grandmother a hug. Then she looked around the crowded bus station. "Where's Tiffany?"

"Her mother called to say she was spending an extra hour at her dance class. Mrs. Parks will drop Tiffany off at our building as soon as she's through," Mrs. Bricker replied.

Tiffany and Stephanie were really close friends

in the second and third grades. We'd all heard about how great Tiffany was: how she wanted to be an actress, and how her older sister Kelly was a model who was on the cover of *Teen* magazine (but Tiffany was a lot more interesting-looking and terrific to be with).

"Oh." Stephanie sounded disappointed.

"Let's get your luggage." Mrs. Bricker led us to the luggage compartment in the side of the bus. The driver had already unloaded all the passengers' bags and set them down on the curb. Stephanie's, Kate's, and Patti's were lined up together, but I didn't see mine at first; it's dark blue denim, with a brown stripe around the edge.

"There it is." Kate pointed. "Down at the end."

I grabbed it, and Mrs. Bricker herded us into the station itself. "We'll get a taxi on Fourth Avenue," she told us.

The building was huge, and it was packed with people: people laughing, people crying because their visitors were leaving, people arguing, people kissing. As we walked around a corner, a person popped up practically in our faces!

"Eeeh!" Patti squeaked.

"It's just a mime," said Stephanie.

His face was painted dead-white, except for thin

black triangles around his eyes and orange lips. He was dressed all in black, and he was wearing white gloves. Without a sound, he motioned for us to stop. Then he started pretending that he was trying to get out of an invisible box, running his gloved hands up the sides of it, looking for a fingerhold. He was so good that I could almost *see* the box.

"Neat!" Kate exclaimed.

Mrs. Bricker dropped some change into a black hat on the floor near him. "We'd better hurry," she told us. "We don't want to leave Tiffany stranded."

"In the city, you never know what's going to happen next!" Stephanie said proudly as the mime bowed to us and waved good-bye.

"Exactly," Patti murmured nervously.

Mrs. Bricker hailed a cab just outside the station. We put our suitcases into the trunk. Then Mrs. Bricker got into the front seat with the cab driver, and the four of us squeezed into the backseat.

"Three sixty-four Merrick Place," Mrs. Bricker told the driver. "And please go through the park."

The park was beautiful, with old-fashioned street lamps lighting the gravel paths, and horse-drawn carriages full of sightseers rolling slowly up the winding road we took. We made a right turn out of the park, drove a few more blocks, and pulled up in front of a big apartment building. A doorman helped Mrs. Bricker out of the cab and unloaded our luggage. "Thank you, Carl," she said.

"Lauren, your suitcase weighs a ton!" Kate said. She'd picked it up to hand it to me. "What have you got in here — rocks?"

It did feel kind of heavy, but I wasn't used to it yet. It was new, a Christmas present from my aunt and uncle. We followed Mrs. Bricker through the long, carpeted lobby and took the elevator to the tenth floor.

"Here we are." Mrs. Bricker unlocked the door to her apartment. "The guest bedroom is down the hall to the left. Why don't you get settled and then come to the kitchen for some snacks?"

"This way." Stephanie led us down the hall and turned on a light. The bedroom was big, with a high ceiling and paintings on the walls. There was a double bed, a chair that folded out into a single bed, and two air mattresses in the closet — "Nana borrowed them from a neighbor," Stephanie explained — for the four of us, plus Tiffany.

"What about this view?" Stephanie pulled the cord on a shade, and we were looking out at the Pequontic River.

"Wow!" Kate and I said.

It's the same old river that runs past Riverhurst, but the Pequontic is about twenty times wider when it reaches the city and flows into the ocean. There were two tugs strung with colored lights chugging upriver towing barges, and a freighter, and an enormous tanker at least a block long. I could have sat there for hours, just looking — if I hadn't been hungry.

"I'm starving," I announced.

Everyone groaned. "So, what else is new?" Kate said.

I ignored them. "Do you think we could go to the kitchen now?"

"The girl has to eat," Stephanie said with a grin. "Like a baby — at least once every two or three hours. Lauren, if you were as short as I am, you'd be three feet wide!"

Luckily, I come from a tall, thin family. Patti's the only girl in our class who's taller than I am.

Mrs. Bricker had a real feast laid out on the kitchen table. "I didn't know what you girls like," she said, "so I got a little of everything at the delicatessen."

She certainly did! There was a three-foot-long hero sandwich with salami, cheese, ham, tomatoes, and lettuce to share; a plate of stuffed eggs decorated with pimiento; a big bowl of potato salad; potato chips — barbecue *and* onion and sour cream flavored; cheese dip; and fruit salad.

"The sodas are on the counter, and the chocolate fudge cake is in the refrigerator," Mrs. Bricker added. "Please help yourselves. Call me if you need anything."

"Yummy!" I murmured, grabbing a plate.

But we'd hardly made a dent in the food supply when the doorbell rang and Stephanie rushed to answer it.

Chapter
2

"Tiffany!" we heard Stephanie yell all the way from the front door. "You look fabulous!"

The answer was too low for us to understand.

"We're hanging out in the kitchen. Come meet my friends," Stephanie said. She burst into the kitchen, her eyes sparkling. "Hey, guys, this is Tiffany Parks! Doesn't she look great? Tiffany, this is Kate Beekman, Lauren Hunter, and Patti Jenkins."

"Hello, Tiffany," we all said at the same time.

"Hello," Tiffany replied, giving us the once-over.

"We've heard so much about you," I added.

"Oh?" she said coolly. Tiffany was small and slender, with pale skin and a pointy face and eyebrows that reminded me of a cat. She had thick, straight, black hair that was parted on the side and hung down to the middle of her back.

Her dark eyes had finished sizing us up. Then they flicked over to Stephanie. "Why in the world did you cut your hair?" Tiffany asked in her husky voice.

"Oh." Stephanie giggled and pulled on her short curls self-consciously. "It's a long story. We wanted to have a surprise party for Kate's birthday, and Lauren and Patti and I — "

"It makes you look about six years old," Tiffany interrupted her. "And *where* did you get that sweater?"

Stephanie was wearing a handknit sweater in her favorite color combination — red, black, and white. She'd bought it at Dandelion, a store on Main Street, one Saturday when the four of us went shopping together.

Stephanie looked down at her sweater, then up at Tiffany. "Uh, Riverhurst," she answered.

Tiffany nodded knowingly.

Kate raised an eyebrow at me. I couldn't believe it, either. Stephanie was not the type to let anyone push her around.

Tiffany put her tote bag down and took off her coat. Underneath it, she was wearing bright blue sweat pants over a purple leotard. She stood on her tiptoes and stretched her arms up in the air, slowly, one at a time. "My shoulder muscles tightened up in the cold after all that dancing." It was more of an announcement than an explanation.

"I thought you were interested in being an actress, Tiffany," Kate said, "not a dancer."

"An actress has to know how to dance," Tiffany answered. "And sing. I take voice lessons, too."

"She has a wonderful voice," Stephanie put in.

"Do you think Bonnie Lorenzo can dance and sing?" I wondered. Bonnie Lorenzo is one of my favorite actresses of all time.

"*Who* is Bonnie Lorenzo?" Tiffany asked snootily.

"She's on *Dark Valley*," I replied. When I saw the blank look on Tiffany's face, I added, "One of the soaps."

Tiffany smirked. "I'm talking about real actresses. You know, ones who can actually act?"

"Well, excu-u-use me," Kate murmured.

"Tiffany, would you like something to eat?" Patti said quickly. She's good at heading off arguments between Stephanie and Kate, and we could both tell from the gleam in Kate's eye that she wasn't really taken with Tiffany.

"The potato salad is great," I said loudly and enthusiastically.

Tiffany looked at all the food on the kitchen

table, and the corners of her mouth curled down. "Totally fatty and greasy," she pronounced. "Yucky for my skin."

"What about the fruit salad?" Stephanie suggested. She spooned some into a bowl and handed it to Tiffany, who took it without a thank-you, peered at it suspiciously, and decided the strawberries were safe.

Kate hadn't been sidetracked, however. "What do you mean by a real actress, Tiffany?" she asked.

"A *real* actress, as opposed to TV actresses, or most of the ones in the movies," Tiffany replied. She chewed slowly on a melon ball before she continued, "An actress trained on the *stage*."

Stephanie nodded. "Tiffany's already been in several plays," she said, proud of her friend.

"School plays?" I asked, serving myself more of the fatty, greasy potato salad.

Tiffany smiled a superior smile and waited for Stephanie to answer for her: "No, real plays in real theaters! She was Catherine in *Moon Over Twelfth Street,* and Lucy in *Three in the Afternoon*."

"*Three for the Afternoon*," Tiffany corrected her sternly.

"I've never heard of them," Kate muttered to me.

"Neither have I," I whispered back. I get such

awful stage fright that just the idea of being in a play gives me an upset stomach. I cut another piece of hero to settle my nerves. "This is just about the best hero I've ever eaten," I said to Stephanie.

"*Best!* Remember 'Bests'?" she exclaimed to Tiffany.

"Oh, Stephanie . . ." Tiffany drawled disdainfully.

"Bests?" said Kate.

"It was kind of a game we used to play. We'd always start out with 'best friend,' and Tiffany would say 'Stephanie,' and I'd say 'Tiffany.' Then we'd go on to 'best party,' or 'best ice cream,' or 'best store.' "

"The best party ever was Kate's surprise party," Patti said, getting the ball rolling.

"What about best ice cream? The Banana Boats at Charlie's," I said.

"No ice cream is better than the stuff at Scrumptious," said Stephanie. "We'll eat there tomorrow while we're sight-seeing. You're going with us, aren't you, Tiffany?" she added.

"Oh — uh — I guess so," Tiffany said. "Sure." But she didn't look sure at all.

"Best trip will definitely be this one," I said hopefully.

Mrs. Bricker walked into the kitchen then. "Hello, Tiffany. How have you been, dear?"

"Hello, Mrs. Bricker." Tiffany gave her a toothy grin — it was the first time we had seen her smile. "Very well, thank you."

"I thought you girls might enjoy renting some movies," Mrs. Bricker said. "I belong to a video club that delivers. Would you like to look at their list?"

"Thanks, Nana." Stephanie took the green booklet, and the rest of us crowded around to read over her shoulder.

"Wow! Lots of old movies . . . and two whole pages of foreign films!" Kate exclaimed. "Fantastic! I've always wanted to see this Swedish movie, *Raspberries in Fall*. Bjorn Bergstrom was the director."

"*Raspberries in Fall* it is," said Mrs. Bricker. "Any other requests?"

"What about *Mare's Nest*?" I asked. "It's an old 1930s comedy with the Fabulous Flynn Brothers."

"It's lots of fun. I saw it when I was a girl," Mrs. Bricker told us. "Anything else?"

"*Aardvarks*," said Tiffany. "They filmed the original play."

"Fine. I'll call up right now," Mrs. Bricker said. "The VCR is in the living room. Stephanie, please take in the drinks. And there's a large bag of those cheese things you like in the pantry."

Movies were a great idea! We couldn't be talking to each other because we'd be watching them, so

16

Tiffany wouldn't be able to get Kate annoyed enough to jump on her case. Three movies would last at least four hours, and then we'd be too tired to argue. We'd have made it safely through the sleepover . . . or so I thought.

We moved into the living room with Dr. Peppers (club soda for Tiffany) and Cheese Doodles (celery sticks for Tiffany) and fudge cake (nothing for Tiffany). Is life really worth living without fudge cake? By the time we were set up, the delivery boy had come with the three movies, since the video store was just across the street.

"We'll watch *Aardvarks* first," Stephanie said brusquely. She snapped it into the VCR. Tiffany nodded, as if to say it was the only one of the three worth seeing.

I thought a play named *Aardvarks* had to have something about animals in it, but I was wrong. Three people sat on stools on an empty stage and talked about death. I can definitely say it was the most boring seventy minutes I've ever spent in front of a TV screen. Kate, Patti, and I were polite about it, but by the time it was over I was ready to scream.

"Very powerful," Tiffany said solemnly as "The End" flashed onto the screen.

"Very," Stephanie agreed, equally solemnly.

Kate nudged me and rolled her eyes.

"Really moving," said Tiffany.

"It almost moved me right out of the room," Kate murmured in my ear.

I managed to turn a snicker into a sneeze.

"Let's watch the Swedish movie next," Patti suggested.

Stephanie clicked in the cassette, and Kate put on her glasses to read the subtitles. (She's a little nearsighted.) In the first scene, we were looking at an enormous mansion near a lake. A girl in a long white dress stood at an open window. Beside her was a handsome young officer in a blue uniform with lots of gold braid. They spoke — in Swedish, of course. That's when Tiffany started to complain.

"What a drag!" Tiffany said. "I hate subtitles."

Kate gives all movies, including bad ones, her full attention. It drives her crazy when people talk during a movie. She doesn't even like it when you talk over the commercials they slip into TV movies.

"It's like butting in while somebody else is saying something," Kate explained to me once. "It's bad manners."

"Sssh!" she said to Tiffany now.

Tiffany humphed. "Why should I be quiet? You can read what they're saying." She turned to Stephanie. "Remember Myra Dillard from school?"

Stephanie glanced at Kate a little warily. "Yes," she whispered.

But Tiffany didn't bother to lower *her* voice. "She's lost a lot of weight, permed her hair, and she's singing in a rock band with some seventh-graders. She thinks she's so cool!"

"Do you mind?" Kate said grimly. She switched off the VCR and glared at Tiffany.

"What *is* your problem? You can't understand Swedish!" Tiffany glared right back at her.

"Are all kids from the city as rude as you are?" Kate said then. "Or did we just get lucky?"

Tiffany was dumbstruck. "Wha-a-a-t?" she practically shrieked. "Stephanie!"

"Kate! Tiffany. . . ." Stephanie looked back and forth from one to the other.

"You're actually going to let her talk to me like that, aren't you!" Tiffany stood up, her eyes flashing. "You've really changed, Stephanie. You're turning into a total hick, just like them!"

Tiffany flounced out of the living room, grabbed her tote bag and coat from the kitchen, and marched down the hall to the front door.

"Tiffany, where are you going?" Stephanie asked anxiously, running after her.

"Home!" Tiffany thundered. She flung open the door and slammed it shut behind her.

Chapter 3

By the time Stephanie got the door open and dashed out into the hall, the elevator doors were closing. "Thanks a lot, Kate!" Stephanie muttered through her teeth.

"Thanks a lot, *Kate?*" Kate spluttered. "She was impossible!"

"Stephanie, did I hear the door slam?" Mrs. Bricker stepped out of her bedroom in a bathrobe and slippers. She glanced at the four of us, then looked around for a fifth. "Where is Tiffany?"

"She left, Nana," Stephanie answered. "She said she was going home."

"By herself, in this city, at ten-thirty at night? Maybe Carl can stop her in the lobby." Mrs. Bricker pushed a button and spoke into the intercom. "Carl? Are you there? It's Mrs. Bricker in 10B."

"Yes, Mrs. Bricker." The doorman's voice

crackled up from the intercom in the lobby.

"Is one of Stephanie's friends down there? A small girl with long, dark hair?"

"I just put her in a cab, Mrs. Bricker," Carl answered. "She told me she had your permission."

"Oh, dear." Mrs. Bricker shook her head. "Thank you, Carl."

Mrs. Bricker turned to Stephanie. "What happened? Why did Tiffany leave so suddenly?"

Stephanie scowled at Kate. "Well . . ." she began.

Kate spoke up. "Tiffany and I had a disagreement, Mrs. Bricker. I'm sorry."

Mrs. Bricker patted Kate's shoulder distractedly. "I'd better call her mother right away." She hurried back to her bedroom. "Mrs. Parks? Mrs. Bricker," we heard her say. "I just wanted to let you know that Tiffany is on her way home in a taxi. . . . That's right, there was some sort of misunderstanding. . . . Yes. . . . Would you mind terribly calling me back when she gets there? Let us know that she's safely home? Thank you."

Patti, Kate, and I sat down on the living room couch. Stephanie flopped into the armchair. All of us were waiting, none of us was looking at anyone else. I thought about the city outside the windows: it really was kind of scary at night. Five minutes

21

passed . . . ten minutes . . . when the phone finally rang, I jumped a mile.

"Hello?" Mrs. Bricker answered quickly. "Oh, I'm so relieved! Thank you so much for calling. . . . Right. Good night, Mrs. Parks."

"Is she okay, Nana?" Stephanie called out.

"Tiffany's home, getting ready for bed. And I think you girls ought to think about going to bed yourselves." Mrs. Bricker walked back into the living room. "You must be tired from your trip."

Stephanie kissed her grandmother, then trudged toward the guest bedroom.

"Good night, Mrs. Bricker," Patti and I said.

"I'm sorry," Kate repeated as we filed out. "I shouldn't have argued with Tiffany."

"Tiffany takes herself very seriously," Mrs. Bricker told her. "Perhaps a little *too* seriously."

So Mrs. Bricker wasn't really angry about it. But Stephanie sure was.

"I guess I shouldn't have yelled at your friend, Stephanie, even if she was being horrible," Kate said when she walked into the bedroom.

"You're just jealous of her!" Stephanie snapped.

"Jealous!" Kate's cheeks turned an angry red. "Of that phony? Get real!"

"What do you mean, phony? Tiffany *is* an actress," Stephanie said.

22

"She's an actress, all right. Everything she does is one big act. 'Stephanie, whatever did you do to your hair?' " Kate imitated Tiffany's husky voice. " 'And those hicky friends — simply too awful.' "

I started to giggle — I couldn't help myself. Even Patti was having a hard time not cracking up.

"Ruining a friendship is pretty funny, huh?" said Stephanie.

But was Tiffany really her friend? I wouldn't want a friend treating me that way.

"Here are the sheets." Stephanie opened the dresser and pulled some out. "I'm sleeping on one of the air mattresses." She dragged it into the corner, away from the rest of us.

"Okay, Lauren, you and Patti should have the bed, because you're tall," Kate directed. "I'll take the fold-out chair."

While Patti and I made up our bed, Kate stared out the window at the building across the way. "It's like an old movie I saw once, where a man solves a murder without ever leaving his apartment, by just looking out the window." She pressed her forehead against the glass and cupped her hands around her eyes. "Wish I could see better."

"There're some binoculars on the desk in the living room," Stephanie muttered. She was lying on her stomach on the air mattress.

"Thanks." I was back with them right away. "What does your grandmother use them for?"

"Nana's a birdwatcher," Stephanie said curtly.

Kate took them, adjusted the focus, and pointed the binoculars at a brightly lighted window on the top floor of the building. "These are really strong! I can a see a man and a woman moving around . . . wow! He's jerking her arm . . . they're fighting!"

"Give me those things!" Stephanie jumped up from the floor to snatch the binoculars from Kate. "Where?"

"Third window from the left," Kate said.

Stephanie zeroed in, focusing, while Patti and I squinted out the window, too. Stephanie didn't say anything for a few seconds. Then she snorted. "They're not fighting — they're dancing! Look, you can even see a music video on the TV behind them."

She handed the binoculars back to Kate. "Oh . . . yeah," Kate said sheepishly. "You're right." But Kate grinned at me — she'd gotten Stephanie talking again.

"Let me take a look." I aimed the binoculars at the windows two floors down. "Somebody's having a dinner party, with candles and everything. And the guy next door to them is lifting weights. Want to see?" I handed the binoculars to Patti.

Patti giggled a little uneasily as she raised them

24

to her eyes. "I feel sort of like a Peeping Tom," she admitted.

"Nana says people who want privacy in a crowded city had better close their curtains," Stephanie told her.

"Oh, there are two cats looking out the window on the fifth floor. I think they're Persians," Patti said. "I wonder what Adelaide is doing right now." Adelaide is Patti's cat, the sister of my cat, Rocky, Stephanie's cat, Cinders, and Kate's cat, Fredericka.

"Let me see." Stephanie took the glasses again. "A third one just jumped up. Aren't they cute?"

At least we weren't going to spend the weekend angry with each other. But there was a lot to write in my journal before bed, so I thought I'd better get started. I laid my suitcase on its side and unzipped it. I pushed back the flap and reached for my journal, which should have been right on top. But it wasn't.

"Maybe it slipped down," I said to myself. I dug under the blue sweater, and felt something hard and heavy. I tugged at it . . . and out came a man's hiking boot! I stuck in my other hand, and pulled out another hiking boot. Then I held up the blue sweater. It had a red stripe and three reindeer on the front.

"Hey!" I said loudly. "These aren't my clothes!"

Chapter
4

"Not your clothes?" Patti kneeled down beside me as I unfolded a pair of brown corduroy pants, a navy turtleneck, and a pair of men's shorts with sailboats on them.

"No, definitely not your clothes," Stephanie said.

Besides my best blue sweater, I'd packed my turquoise-and-black top, my black stretch pants, two pairs of leg warmers, and my silver Reeboks. All of my favorite stuff had gone off with somebody else!

"It must have happened at the bus station," Kate was saying. "Your new suitcase looks exactly like this one."

"Some guy just grabbed the wrong bag," I groaned.

"That's why it was down at the end, instead of lined up together with ours. This suitcase must have

26

been unloaded first, which means it was loaded last, which means the owner must have gotten on the bus after we did," Stephanie said thoughtfully.

"Not necessarily. There were two luggage compartments on our bus. Maybe this was loaded into the first one before our stop, and all our suitcases were loaded into the second compartment because the first one was already full," Kate suggested.

"I'm sure the man will call your house as soon as he discovers he's got a suitcase full of girls' leg warmers and stretch pants," Patti said soothingly. "You have your name on your bag, don't you, Lauren?"

I shook my head in disgust. "I have my name in my old suitcase, and I meant to put it in the new one, but I never got around to it."

"But your journal's in there, right?" Kate asked.

I nodded.

"That's good enough. He'll see your name on the front of your journal, plus Riverhurst Elementary School, and he'll know to call the Hunter family in Riverhurst — "

I shook my head again. "I didn't write my full name on my journal, on purpose. It seemed more private that way."

"And he can't call the school about a Lauren, because it's the weekend." Stephanie was checking out the suitcase on the floor. "Maybe there's a name in this one."

We all started to look. There were no name tags or stickers anywhere on the bag itself. We dug through the side compartments, but all we found was an electric razor and a toothbrush.

"Let's go through his clothes." Kate turned the pockets of the corduroy trousers inside out. She didn't come up with anything but a plain white handkerchief.

Stephanie pulled a checked shirt out of the suitcase. It was brand-new, never been worn. "Adelman's," Stephanie said. "That's a big men's store here. They've probably sold hundreds of shirts like this one."

Patti lifted out the last piece of clothing in the suitcase, a long-sleeved undershirt with no pockets. "Not even a laundry mark," she said.

But at the bottom of the bag was a flat, square box. Kate grabbed it and opened it up. A large wheel of brown tape lay inside it.

"It looks like cassette tape," I said.

"It is, kind of," Patti said. "I remember my father had a big, old reel-to-reel tape recorder. The tape wound off a full reel like this one onto an empty one."

"This might give us a clue about the owner,"

Kate said, tapping the tape. "But where are we going to find an old tape recorder that will play this?"

"Maybe one of Nana's friends has one. We'll ask her first thing in the morning," said Stephanie.

Kate lifted the reel of tape out of the flat box and turned it over. "Hey, look! A name!" she exclaimed.

It was scribbled in marker on the clear plastic reel. All four of us took turns squinting at it under the floor lamp. "I think it says C. Harkness," Patti decided at last.

"We need the phone book — maybe he lives here!" Stephanie said. She dashed down the hall to the kitchen and returned with the city white pages.

" 'Harbison . . . Harder . . . Hardley . . . Hare . . . ' " she read.

"Hare?" Kate asked.

" 'Hare. Hargrove . . .' here it is: 'Harkness.' "

"There are several of them," said Patti. "None with C as the first initial, though."

"We'll call them anyway. Maybe they're related, at least," I said. "Is there another phone in the apartment besides the one in your grandmother's room?" I asked Stephanie.

"On the kitchen wall," Stephanie answered.

Kate glanced at her watch. "It's too late, Lauren. It's almost twelve o'clock."

She was right — this wasn't Riverhurst, where

we knew most of the people in town and they knew us well enough not to be too annoyed by a late phone call. This was the city, where anything could happen on the other end of the telephone line!

Patti had brought two long T-shirts to sleep in, so I borrowed one of them, and we all went to bed.

I didn't sleep very well that night; I dreamed someone stole all my clothes. A scratching noise woke me up early the next morning. It was Kate's pen — she was scribbling away in her journal.

"Hi," she whispered when she saw my eyes were open. "So much happened yesterday, I thought I'd better write it down while it was still fresh."

"Is Mrs. Bricker awake yet?" I whispered back. Stephanie and Patti were still sound asleep.

"I thought I heard somebody in the kitchen a few minutes ago," Kate replied. She put her journal down on the night table. "Let's go see."

Stephanie's grandmother was mixing up a big bowl of blueberry waffle batter. "Good morning, girls!" she said cheerily. "What time did you get to bed last night?"

"Around twelve," Kate answered. "Mrs. Bricker, Lauren lost her clothes."

Mrs. Bricker glanced at the long T-shirt I was wearing and looked puzzled. She was probably wondering how I could have possibly lost my clothes in her apartment. "She has?"

"There was a mix-up of suitcases at the bus station. Somebody must have taken mine by mistake and left me his," I told her. "I didn't notice until we were getting ready for bed."

I explained about finding the tape with the name "C. Harkness" written on it.

"C. Harkness . . ." Mrs. Bricker repeated slowly. "For some reason, that sounds familiar." She shook her head. "Maybe it will come to me."

Patti and Stephanie wandered into the kitchen just then, Stephanie carrying her journal. "Nana, I thought Mrs. Dean might have the kind of tape recorder we need. Or Mr. Culver." Stephanie yawned sleepily.

"I'll find out as soon as breakfast is over," Mrs. Bricker said. "Now, how many for blueberry waffles?"

Chapter
5

Mrs. Bricker's friends didn't own any reel-to-reel tape recorders, but they had friends who might: they would phone around and find out. In the meantime, we could call all the Harknesses in the book.

" 'A. R. Harkness,' " Kate read. " '555-8132.' "

The phone rang and rang. Finally a man answered. "Who is this?" he demanded in a cross, creaky old voice.

"My name is Lauren Hunter. I wondered if you could have possibly picked up the wrong suitcase at the bus station yesterday?"

"Bus station? Bus station? I haven't left the city in twenty years. What would I be doing with a suitcase at the bus station?" He slammed down the phone.

"Thank you for your help," I said to the dial tone.

Patti smiled encouragingly at me.

" 'D. Harkness: 555-5791,' " read Kate.

"Hello," a woman's pleasant voice said on the other end. "This is Daisy."

"Hi. My name is Lauren Hun — "

It was an answering machine. "I'm not answering the phone right now," the message went on. "But I'll be available at noon. Why don't you call me then? Ta Ta."

I hung up, and Kate said, "We'll try her later."

Gloria Harkness didn't answer at all. The phone number listed for Laurence Harkness had been disconnected. When I called N. T. Harkness, a small child said, "Hewwo."

"Hello. Are your mommy and daddy at home?" I could hear grown-ups talking in the background, but it was another kid who grabbed the phone.

"This is Todd." He spoke a little more clearly. "When are you coming over?"

I hadn't even told him who I was yet! "This is Lauren Hunter. Do you know if anybody in your family took a bus trip yesterday?"

"Sure!" the little boy said. "Are you coming over now?"

"Todd, I've asked you not to play with the phone!" a woman scolded.

Todd started to whine, there was a click, and we were disconnected.

"Maybe we should check on N. T. Harkness in person," I said.

Stephanie looked at the address. "Okay. It's not too far from Logan Lane, the shopping street. Maybe we'll catch N. T. and the other Harknesses with Nana after lunch." She wrote down the telephone numbers and addresses for N. T., Laurence, Gloria, and Daisy and handed them to me.

The plan for the morning was to hit some of the stores. Mrs. Bricker was letting us go without her because the shopping area is busy and safe, and Stephanie knows it so well. At one o'clock Stephanie's grandmother would meet us for lunch at Scrumptious, then we would all do some sight-seeing and some Harknessing, then head back to the apartment.

"I haven't decided about this evening," Mrs. Bricker told us. "I tried to get theater tickets, but all the good plays are sold out for weeks in advance. Maybe we'll go to the Sky Rink."

Which brought us back to the subject of clothes. What was I going to wear? I couldn't wear the same old stuff I'd had on the whole day before!

I was too tall for Kate's and Stephanie's things; even their sweaters were too short for me. Patti lent me some dark green stretch pants. Mrs. Bricker sent Stephanie to a store down the street to buy socks and underwear, and she lent me a sweater of her own: gray wool, with flowers and dark green leaves on it.

"Oh, it's really too nice," I said to Mrs. Bricker. "It would be safe to lend it to Kate — she's the neat one. I'm sort of a slob."

But Mrs. Bricker insisted. "Don't worry about it, Lauren. It's washable. You can be as sloppy as you please."

I thought we'd seen the last of Tiffany Parks, for that weekend at least. But while the rest of us were getting ready to go out, I heard Stephanie call her on the phone in the kitchen.

"Hello, Mrs. Parks? This is Stephanie Green. May I speak to Tiffany? . . . Hi, Tiffany" — Stephanie lowered her voice — "I'm really sorry about last night. Sometimes Kate gets a little . . . right . . . umm-hmm. She doesn't really mean it. . . . Yeah. . . . Listen, do you want to go around with us today? Do the stores? Oh . . . I know. . . . Well, what about tonight? Nana's taking us to dinner and skating at the Sky Rink. . . . Really? Terrific! Why don't you come over at about seven. . . . Okay, see you then!"

Stephanie didn't really meet my eye when she came back into the bedroom. "Tiffany," she mumbled, putting her journal down on the night table. "Maybe she'll come to dinner with us tonight."

"Great," I said, not at all enthusiastically.

Stephanie changed the subject. "Patti, don't you have any old city friends you want to call?"

"I left my first school so long ago that I'm sure nobody remembers me," Patti told her. "And my closest friend at the second school, Amy Winter, moved to Maine last year. Thanks anyway."

Kate was the last one dressed, looking as neat as always, not a single blond hair out of place. "Ready?" she said.

"Let's hit the trail," Stephanie said cheerfully. She was feeling much better about Tiffany. Stephanie picked up her journal, and Kate stuck hers in her pocketbook.

"Good-bye, Nana," Stephanie called. "See you at Scrumptious at one."

Mrs. Bricker joined us at the front door. "Have a good time. Be careful."

We rode down in the elevator, said hello to the day doorman, Willie, and hurried up the street toward the bus stop. There was a note taped to two of the lampposts we passed: "MISSING — brown male dog, small terrier-type. Weighs about fifteen pounds, two years old, wearing red collar. Answers to the name *MAX*. If seen, or if you have any information, please call 555-4033. REWARD.''

''Poor thing,'' Patti murmured. ''Dogs get so scared when they're lost.''

''Maybe you could hang up some signs about your suitcase, Lauren,'' Kate said.

''You'd have every weirdo in the city calling you up — not a good idea,'' said Stephanie. ''Here comes our bus. Run!''

Chapter
6

The bus stopped every four blocks or so to let people on or off, and there was so much dodging in and out of traffic that I thought I was going to get carsick. But the bus did take us right to Logan Lane in the middle of the city. We got off in front of a huge toy store named Rumpelstiltskin.

"Cute name," I said. "Look at that stuffed giraffe!" We crowded up to the front window.

"It's practically life-size!" Kate exclaimed.

"My dad used to bring me here when I was little," Patti said. "Can we go in for a minute?"

"Sure, we have plenty of time before lunch," Stephanie replied.

We saw a set of Tinkertoys large enough to climb on, a robot that answered questions, a miniature yellow Corvette convertible that you could drive twenty-five miles an hour, and a doll named Testy Tess who had tantrums.

"Let's get out of here — she reminds me too much of Melissa," Kate said over the doll's screeching. Melissa is Kate's bratty little sister.

We went next door into a fancy dress shop called Nell's. There weren't that many dresses hanging out where you could see them, but each one was beautiful.

"This is a gorgeous formal," Stephanie exclaimed. "I can just see myself in it four years from now." It was black velvet with a red sash.

Kate turned her head sideways to read the price tag. "And it's yours for only three thousand two hundred and fifty dollars!" she gasped.

"Don't even breathe on it!" I warned. "You might have to buy it, and it would take you *forty* years to save enough allowance!"

We left in a hurry without touching anything and went around the corner to a pet store. Three poodle puppies frolicked in the window. Inside there were more puppies, and a whole bunch of glass terrariums full of creepy-crawlies like lizards, and snakes, and even tarantulas! Patti bought a tiny striped lizard for her little brother, Horace, and I got a ball with a bell in it for my kitten, Rocky.

Stephanie checked her watch. "Hey, it's almost one. We'd better hurry."

Scrumptious was at the end of the next block, in a narrow, three-story building painted chocolate-brown and white. It was neat inside, with strange wooden sculptures that looked like huge clocks on the walls, and old trumpets and cowboy boots and moose heads hanging from the ceiling.

"There's Nana," Stephanie said. "At the round table in the back."

"What have you seen that was interesting?" Mrs. Bricker asked as we plopped down on the old-fashioned wicker chairs.

We told her about the robot, and the black velvet dress, and the tarantulas, and Patti opened the cardboard container to show her Horace's lizard. Then we checked out the enormous Scrumptious menu. I ended up ordering a grilled cheese sandwich, which doesn't sound very special, but it was, and a strawberry ice-cream soda called "Berry Best."

We were waiting for our dessert — we were splitting a chocolate mousse for four, and Mrs. Bricker was having cappuccino, which is foamy coffee with cinnamon in it — when I said, "I wish I had my journal. I'm going to forget half the things we've done today."

"Use a page out of mine." Stephanie took her journal out of her shoulder bag and opened it up to tear a page out. "Wait a second — this isn't mine," she said. "It's . . ." Stephanie stopped talking and started reading to herself. Suddenly her face froze. " 'I never would have believed it, but when she's around Tiffany, Stephanie turns into a real wimp!' " she said in a strangled voice. Stephanie slammed the journal down on the table. "Friends like you make Tiffany look pretty good, Kate Beekman!" She jumped up from her chair and stormed out of the restaurant.

"Stephanie!" Mrs. Bricker scooted her chair back and started after her granddaughter.

"Is this getting to be a habit, or what?" I wondered out loud. First Tiffany, and now Stephanie. "What was she talking about?"

Kate picked up the journal and looked at the page Stephanie had been reading. "Uh-oh," she muttered.

"That's your journal, and you wrote something about Stephanie in it?" I asked Kate.

She handed me the notebook with a sigh.

" 'I never would have believed it, but when she's around Tiffany, Stephanie turns into a real wimp. And I've never met such a self-centered, stuck-up phony,' " I read. " 'No wonder Stephanie had such an attitude when she first moved to Riverhurst. It'll take us weeks to get her back to normal after this trip.' Oh, Kate!" I groaned.

"Tiffany made me really angry, and I was just letting off steam. Mrs. Mead said a journal's the perfect place to do that," Kate defended herself. "How did I know Stephanie was going to read it?"

"She must have picked up the wrong one off the night table," Patti said with a worried frown.

Now what? It was only Saturday afternoon. We had the rest of the city sleepover to get through, not to mention my suitcase to find. But, even more important: It was beginning to seem as though this might be the end of the Sleepover Friends.

Mrs. Bricker was back, looking flustered. "I'll put Stephanie in a cab," she said, taking Stephanie's coat off the back of her chair. "Then we'll have our dessert, and I'll take you three — "

"Wouldn't you like to go with Stephanie?" Patti suggested in her soft voice. "Kate and Lauren and I could take a look at the Historical Society Museum — it's just at the end of the street — and then we'll catch a cab straight back to your apartment."

Mrs. Bricker's face brightened. "Well . . . there are three of you, so it should be safe enough."

"And I've been to the historical museum lots of times," Patti reassured her.

42

Mrs. Bricker nodded. "Perhaps that would be best — Stephanie seems a little upset."

She handed Patti a twenty-dollar bill. "Here's some money for the cab. I'll pay for lunch in front. Please take your time, and we'll see you at home."

"Mrs. Bricker?" Patti said.

"Yes, dear?"

"Would you mind taking the lizard with you?" Patti asked.

"Certainly." And she hurried out, carrying a container of striped lizard.

Our waiter set a huge bowl of chocolate mousse down in the center of the table and served it into four smaller bowls. Then he dumped a big spoonful of whipped cream on top of each of them. *"Bon appétit,"* he said to the three of us.

For once, however, I had no *appétit* at all.

Chapter
7

After lunch, Kate, Patti, and I stood outside Scrumptious and talked things over.

"Maybe we should go back to the apartment and see about Stephanie," Patti said.

"I think we should give her some time to cool off first," said Kate.

"That's probably a good idea," I agreed, although I wasn't too sure Stephanie *was* going to cool off.

"Let's go to the museum, then," Patti said.

We walked down Logan Lane to the end. The Historical Society Museum was in a gray stone building with a bronze statue of a pioneer and his Indian guide out front. We climbed the long flight of marble steps, only to discover the doors were locked.

Kate peered through the thick glass to read a notice on an easel inside. "It's closed for renovations for the next two weeks."

"We'd better find a cab, in that case." Patti was scanning the street.

"Wait a second. Mrs. Bricker's barely had time to get home," I told her. "And Stephanie said N. T. Harkness's apartment is near here. . . . Why not check it out?"

"It wouldn't take long." Kate backed me up.

"I don't know . . . ," Patti said doubtfully. "Do you have the address, Lauren?"

I took the list of Harknesses out of my pocketbook. "N. T.," I murmured. "Forty-nine West Fairview."

"That *is* close," Patti said. "I guess it's all right."

She and Kate and I hurried the three blocks to a small brick apartment building with an awning out front. We pushed open the glass door and found the name Harkness next to a number 11 on the wall inside. Patti pressed the buzzer underneath it, and we waited, ready to explain our business over the intercom. No one asked. A bell suddenly rang, and Patti quickly shoved the inner door open.

Apartment eleven was on the third floor at the back. A little redheaded boy about four or five was looking down the hallway toward us.

"Hi! I'm Todd!" he shouted when he saw us. "Come on in. Hurry!" he called over his shoulder as he raced inside the apartment.

We could hear other kids yelling somewhere in there, although we didn't see anyone when we peeked in. There was a tricycle in the living room, along with a plastic spaceship, some wooden blocks, and a soccer ball.

Kate shrugged. "It looks safe enough to me." She stepped through the door, so Patti and I did, too.

"Company!" Todd was shouting.

Two more small boys rushed in, one younger than Todd, one probably a little older. The youngest grabbed my hand, Todd grabbed Patti's, and they dragged us farther into the apartment.

"Did I hear somebody at the door?" A woman walked into the living room carrying a baby and was pretty surprised to find three strangers standing there. "Who are you?" she exclaimed.

"I'm Lauren, this is Patti, and this is Kate. Are you N. T. Harkness?" I asked her.

"That's my husband," she answered.

"I phoned earlier," I told her. I explained about the mixed-up suitcases. "Did your husband take a bus trip yesterday and come home with the wrong suitcase?" I finally asked.

Mrs. Harkness laughed. "I'm afraid not. Neither

46

of us has been anywhere since the kids got the chicken pox."

"Is that what the spots are?" Kate asked.

I hadn't noticed them before, but the little boy I was holding hands with had pale pink spots on his face and arms. I dropped his hand. "Chicken pox?"

Mrs. Harkness nodded. "Todd's are fading, and so are Andrew's, but Sam has just started to break out. I've tried to keep them away from other kids until they aren't contagious, so they've been just desperate for company. Yesterday they invited in the mailman."

"Do you know how long it takes to come down with chicken pox?" I asked weakly. "I've never had them."

"About two weeks," Mrs. Harkness said. "Good luck with your suitcase," she added as I backed into the hall.

"Thank you." This weekend was turning into a disaster!

"I'm too old for a childhood disease!" I moaned to Kate and Patti outside.

"You're probably immune," Kate said. "Or you would have gotten them when I did."

To cheer me up, Patti said, "We'll try one more Harkness. I have a feeling we'll find your bag at Daisy's."

47

We hopped on a bus for two stops, then got off and walked again. Daisy Harkness still wasn't at home. I left my name, Mrs. Bricker's number, and a message about the suitcase with the doorman.

Gloria Harkness's building was at the end of another bus ride. A woman who was coming in with her groceries told us that Gloria was in Europe for the winter.

Patti really knew her way around, but by the time we got to Laurence Harkness's address, I was thoroughly confused and tired. And there was a sign on Laurence's mailbox: *Moved to Florida*.

"So that's that," I said, totally discouraged. I sank down on a park bench. "I'll never see my turquoise-and-black sweater again. Not to mention my new Reeboks."

Kate sat down on one side of me, and Patti on the other. "See that brown brick building at the end of the next street?" Patti said. "That's the school I went to with Stephanie, the Lucretia Mott School."

"It is?" I perked up, and so did Kate. "Let's take a look at it!" Kate said.

It was much prettier than I expected a city school to be, with a large courtyard in the center planted in grass and shrubs and trees, and a birdbath to one side with its base in the shape of a dolphin. We couldn't get in, because there was a wrought-iron gate across the entrance. But we looked in between the bars of the gate while Patti pointed out the windows of her kindergarten and first-grade classrooms.

A voice interrupted her. "Excuse me — aren't you Patti Jenkins?"

All three of us turned around to face a girl about my height, with curly light brown hair and horn-rimmed glasses.

Patti nodded.

"Remember me? Myra Dillard," the girl said, smiling. "In first grade?"

The Myra Dillard who, according to Tiffany, sang with a rock band?

"Of course!" Patti said then. "I'm surprised you remember *me*."

"You were always nice to me," Myra said. "Even when I was fat. I was really sorry when you moved."

"You live near here, don't you?" said Patti.

"Right across the street," Myra replied.

"These are my friends Lauren Hunter and Kate Beekman," Patti told her.

"Hi, Lauren — Kate," said Myra. "Where do all of you go to school?"

"Oh, we don't live in the city. We live in Riverhurst," Kate said. "We're just visiting for the weekend."

"I was on my way home," Myra said. "Would

you like to come up to my apartment? Have a Coke or something?"

"We'd better not. We're staying with Stephanie Green's grandmother, and she's expecting us," Patti said.

"Stephanie Green," said Myra. "That's right, she moved to Riverhurst, too. Well, maybe we could get together tomorrow — with Stephanie," she suggested.

"I'd like that," Patti said. Kate and I nodded.

"Why don't you call me in the morning?" said Myra. "My number's in the phone book — I have my own line."

"Great! We'll talk to you then," Patti said. We waved good-bye.

"I liked her a lot," I said to Patti. "Why didn't you say you knew her when Tiffany was talking about her?"

Patti shrugged. "I didn't want to argue with Stephanie's friend."

"Anybody Tiffany Parks doesn't like has to be okay," Kate said. "I hope we see her tomorrow."

"The bus stops just around the corner," Patti told us.

"I don't know if my stomach can take more stopping and starting," I said.

"This bus makes only limited stops," Patti promised. "And it ends up on Merrick Place, Mrs. Bricker's street."

We waited across from a park. Kids were flying kites, there was a man selling balloons, and a crowd had gathered to watch a juggler.

"Here's the bus," Patti announced. She walked up the steps, expecting us to follow her on.

"Look, Kate, it's the mime we saw Friday night!" I exclaimed, running around the back of the bus to see better. Kate was right behind me . . .

. . . and the bus and Patti left without us!

I saw Patti's horrified face staring at us through a bus window. Her mouth was moving, but I couldn't hear a word. "Maybe we can catch it at the next bus stop!" I said, racing up the street after the bus.

I ran, and ran . . . and ran, until I heard Kate yelling, "I'm not going another step! It's *limited stops*, Lauren!"

I had forgotten. I skidded to a stop and turned around to see Kate limping toward me, practically collapsing. "Not everybody is as much of a jock as you are," she gasped. "And my legs are half as long as yours." Kate exaggerates about how short she is.

"At least we're not going to get lost," I said. "We'll take the next bus we can get on, and end up on Merrick Place."

"Not yet," Kate said. "I'm not moving until I

catch my breath." She leaned against a parked car and moaned, or at least I thought she did, until she said, "What are you moaning about? You aren't even breathing hard!"

"That wasn't me," I said, trying to figure out where the noise had come from. I looked into the parked car, but it was empty. "Listen, there it is again." It was a kind of weak, whimpering sound.

"Maybe it's *under* the car," I said, since that was the only place left. I got down on my hands and knees and peered between the tires. The sun was starting to set, so it was pretty gloomy under there, but I saw two shiny eyes looking back at me.

"Kate!" I said. "It's a dog."

Chapter
8

"A dog?" Kate joined me on her hands and knees on the sidewalk.

"Here, puppy. Come, puppy," we called gently.

The dog whined again, but he didn't move.

"Maybe he's sick," I said.

"Well, he's scared, that's for sure," said Kate. "Come on, puppy. We're trying to help you."

The dog whimpered and thumped his tail a few times.

"I'm going to crawl under there and get him," I told Kate. "Hold my jacket."

I was halfway under the car when Kate yelled, "Mrs. Bricker's sweater!"

"Too late now," I muttered as I inched across the grimy pavement, squeezing closer to the dog.

I still couldn't see him very well in the shadows, but he was a small dog, with wiry hair and a stumpy tail that he wagged weakly. I stretched out my hand to let him sniff my fingers.

"Careful," Kate warned, her head under the car. "He might bite if he's frightened."

But the dog licked my hand a couple of times. "Okay," I said over my shoulder to Kate, "I'm going to pull him out now."

I reached out with both hands and clutched him around his middle. The dog yelped and squirmed, but he didn't growl. Slowly, I wriggled out backward, holding on to him tightly.

"Farther — just a little farther," Kate directed. "All right — now I can grab him." She reached under the car and lifted the dog out.

I crawled out the rest of the way and sat up. "Wow, is he a mess!" He was so dirty I couldn't even tell what color he was, and he was as thin as a rail.

"This city's not the cleanest place, and he's probably been on the street for a while," Kate said. When she patted the dog, he yelped again. "Lauren, I think his back leg is hurt."

"It looks kind of swollen," I said, squinting at it in the fading light. "Maybe it's just bruised."

"He's starting to shiver," Kate said. "What are we going to do with him?"

"Here, wrap him up in my jacket," I said, taking

it off the car hood, where Kate had laid it. "We're going to carry him back to Mrs. Bricker's." How, though? It was too far to walk, and we couldn't get on a bus with a dirty little dog.

"No problem, I'll get us a cab," said Kate.

Kate handed me the dog, stepped out into the street, and held up her hand. In a minute or two she'd hailed a cab, just like a city person!

But the cab driver wasn't wild about the idea of a dog in his car.

"I'll hold him," I promised, "so he won't bother anything. You won't even know he's here."

"Please?" Kate pleaded.

The driver sighed. "Get in, get in. Where do you wanna go?"

Kate opened the back door and we jumped in. "Three sixty-four Merrick Place," she said. "And step on it!" Kate whispered to me, "I've always wanted to say that."

With the dog on our minds, we hadn't given much thought to Patti, speeding uptown on the bus. But she hadn't forgotten about us. We'd gone about two blocks in the cab when I spotted her out the window, jogging down the sidewalk past us.

"Wait, Patti!" I yelled out the window. "Please stop!" I said to the cab driver.

"This isn't Merrick Place," he argued.

"But that's our friend!" Kate told him.

"Two kids, a dog, another kid . . ." grumbled the driver. "What next?" But he pulled over to the curb so Patti could climb in.

"I was trying to tell you to stay there . . . that I would come back for you . . . but you couldn't hear me . . ." Patti puffed as the cab pulled back out into traffic. ". . . a dog?"

"We found him under a car," Kate said. "He's half-starved, and his leg is hurt."

"Maybe it's the dog on the lamppost!" Patti exclaimed.

The dog on the lamppost? I didn't know what she was talking about.

"You know, the lost dog!" Patti said. "Is he brown?"

"He might be," I said, opening up my jacket a little. "He'll have to have a bath before we can tell."

"Is he wearing a red collar?" asked Patti.

I parted the matted hair on the dog's neck. "Uh . . . yeah! It *is* red. But his tags must have fallen off. All that's left is the little hook."

"What was that dog's name?" Kate was trying to remember.

"Max!" Patti said.

I thought the little dog's ears twitched when he heard it.

56

"Max, is that you?" I asked him.

He cocked his head and looked up at me.

"We'll call the number on the notice when we get back to the apartment," Kate said. "That lost dog might have been found already."

"And if it has?" asked Patti. "What will we do with this one?"

"Maybe Rocky and Bullwinkle" — Bullwinkle is my family's big, old dog — "will have a new pal from the city," I replied, stroking the dog's nose.

As soon as we'd paid the cab driver and climbed out in front of Mrs. Bricker's building, Patti ran down the street to pull the number off the lamppost.

"I hope Mrs. Bricker doesn't mind animals," Kate said while we were riding the elevator up to ten.

"I hope she doesn't mind grease on her nice sweater," I added glumly. In the bright light I could see a dark streak down the front of the sweater that was definitely not a part of the pattern.

Mrs. Bricker opened her front door a second after we rang the bell. "Come in, girls. I'm so glad you're home. I was starting to worry," she greeted us. Before we had to explain about the museum, and admit that we'd been wandering all over town, she went on, "Good news! A friend brought over a tape recorder for your tape. Stephanie is trying to make it work." Mrs. Bricker looked at me more closely. "What have you got in your coat, Lauren?"

"We found a stray dog, Mrs. Bricker." I pulled my bundled-up jacket open to show her, while Kate told her about the notice on the lamppost.

"Isn't he darling!" Mrs. Bricker said as the dog cocked his head at her and thumped his tail. "Poor little thing, I'll bet he's hungry. Let me see what I can rustle up for him in the kitchen."

"Where's Stephanie?" I whispered to Patti.

Patti shrugged her shoulders and pointed down the hall toward the guest bedroom.

We followed Mrs. Bricker into the kitchen, Kate holding the dog while I dialed the number on the notice.

"Hello?" said a woman's voice on the other end of the line.

"Hello, are you the person who's lost the dog?" I asked.

"Have you found Max?" the woman practically shrieked.

"Maybe," I said. "Could you come over and take a look?"

"Absolutely! Where are you?"

I gave her Mrs. Bricker's address.

"I'm just a few blocks away. I'll be right there!" the woman said.

Chapter 9

We didn't have long to wait. When the doorbell rang, Stephanie's grandmother answered it. We heard her talking to the woman for a while before Mrs. Bricker finally said, "Right through here. The dog is in the kitchen." She walked through the door: "Girls, meet Elizabeth Hatch. She and I have shared a bench in the park several times, but we've never actually introduced ourselves. Elizabeth, this is Kate Beekman, Patti Jenkins, Lauren — "

"Max!" yelled Elizabeth Hatch as soon as she spotted him.

Max had been lapping up a big bowl of hamburger meat and egg that Mrs. Bricker had mixed up for him. But as soon as Elizabeth spoke, he dashed across the floor on three legs, and she scooped him up.

"I have a feeling it's Max," Kate said.

Elizabeth Hatch was younger than my mom, with blondish-brown hair in a loose ponytail, and a round, friendly face. She was wearing jeans and a really great suede jacket, but she didn't care how dirty Max was. She was laughing and crying as he licked her chin.

"There's something wrong with his hind leg," I pointed out.

"I'll take him right to the vet," Elizabeth promised.

"How did you lose him?" Kate asked her.

"I'd let him off his leash to run in the park, just as I'd done a hundred times. Max saw a squirrel, he chased it . . . and he disappeared. I looked for him for hours that day. Nothing. I thought he was gone forever." Elizabeth hugged the dog. "You're never getting off that leash again!" Then she looked at us. "I'll never be able to thank you enough. There is a hundred-dollar reward, though."

I shook my head. Elizabeth loved Max so much that it wouldn't be right to take money for finding him.

"We're just glad you've got him back," Kate said, and Patti agreed.

"Maybe I could at least treat you to dinner?" Elizabeth suggested. "What about tomorrow?"

"We're leaving tomorrow afternoon to go back home," Kate told her.

"Oh, you don't live here?"

"We're here for the weekend," I said.

Elizabeth thought for a moment. Then she said, "I do the lighting for a play — *The Body in the Garage*, kind of a mystery-comedy in a small theater downtown. Would you like to watch a performance this evening from backstage?"

"That would be neat!" I exclaimed.

"Great!" said Kate.

"We'd love it," Patti added.

"There are four of us," I told Elizabeth, hoping Stephanie would agree to come with us.

"I can manage that," said Elizabeth. "Would it be all right?" she asked Mrs. Bricker. "Of course I'd pick the girls up and bring them back."

"I think it would be lots of fun for them," Mrs. Bricker said.

Kate and Patti and I saw Elizabeth and Max to the door. I was a little disappointed that he wasn't going home with me.

"I'll come get you at six forty-five, then," Elizabeth said to us. "Thank you a million times for Max."

The door had hardly closed when Stephanie called out: "Nana? You have to hear this!" She rushed into

61

the hall. Then she noticed us. "Oh, you're back," she said stiffly. Stephanie turned her back on Kate. "Lauren, that tape in the suitcase is very weird."

"What do you mean?" I asked her.

"There's nothing on it until almost at the end. And then . . . come listen to it."

The bulky old tape recorder was plugged in in the guest bedroom. Stephanie hit the fast-forward switch, and the tape spun around. She hit *stop*, then *play*.

"I've asked you nicely, and now I'm telling you," a man's deep voice growled, "keep away from me!"

A woman's voice was so soft that we couldn't make the words out, even with the volume turned way up.

The man spoke again. "Sandra, don't come any closer. . . ."

The woman mumbled something.

"I'm warning you. . . ."

More mumbling.

There was a loud bang — and we'd reached the end of the tape.

Patti and I looked at each other wide-eyed. I gulped. "Was that a gun?!"

Patti gasped. "He shot her!"

Mrs. Bricker was frowning. "I'm sure there's a reasonable explanation for this."

But what was it?

Patti and I thought we should take the tape straight to the nearest police station, but Kate didn't agree. Neither did Stephanie.

"You're always jumping to conclusions, Lauren," Stephanie said.

Kate added, "You and Patti are letting your imaginations run away with you. Is a murderer really going to make a tape of the crime, and then" — she pointed to the big hiking boots lying on the floor next to the open suitcase — "take it on a hiking trip?"

That did sound kind of silly. Still, was my turquoise-and-black sweater in the hands of a hardened criminal?

One thing was certain — the tape hadn't gotten us any closer to finding my clothes. Which brought me to another urgent problem: what was I going to wear that night? I'd wrecked Mrs. Bricker's sweater, and the stretch pants that Patti had lent me weren't in such great shape after their trip under a car.

Mrs. Bricker was staring at the reel of tape and murmuring, "C. Harkness, C. Harkness," to herself, but she snapped out of it to tell me not to worry: "I ran the clothes you had on yesterday through the wash, Lauren. They're ready to wear to the theater."

"What theater?" Stephanie asked me.

I filled her in about the lost dog, adding, "We're

63

all going to watch *The Body in the Garage* from backstage. Max's owner invited the four of us."

Stephanie frowned. "I'm afraid I won't be going."

"Why not?" I asked. I lowered my voice. "Come on, Stephanie, Kate didn't really mean what she wrote. She was just upset."

"Tiffany's coming over this evening," said Stephanie.

I'd completely forgotten.

Chapter
10

"We can't really bring a fifth person, can we?" I said. "Four kids are already a lot to have standing around backstage."

"You're probably right," Stephanie said.

Kate was back in the kitchen, but Patti spoke up. "Then we won't go, either," she said. "We've got Elizabeth's number — we'll just call her up and tell her — "

"No, that's okay," Stephanie interrupted. "Tiffany's probably already seen the play anyway. She and Nana and I will have dinner out, and then we'll go skating at the Sky Rink."

"Are you sure?" I asked her.

"I'm sure," said Stephanie. "It'll be just like old times." Before the Sleepover Friends — and maybe Stephanie preferred it that way.

Patti and Kate and I had to eat in a hurry — tuna sandwiches on toast — and dress in a hurry, because it was practically time for Elizabeth to come back for us. Then Horace's lizard escaped while we were feeding him a dead fly: We finally found him under the bedspread. Then the doorbell rang, and it was time for us to go.

I thought Stephanie looked a little sad as we rushed out the door. "Have a good time," she said to Patti and me; she still wasn't talking to Kate.

We had a terrific time! *The Body in the Garage* was at an old theater with plaster cupids across the front, called the Sturgis. We went in through the back door (it's called the stage door) with the actors and stagehands. I had expected backstage to be a madhouse, with people running here and there shouting orders and shoving scenery around, and actors half in and half out of costume slapping makeup on their faces. But it wasn't like that at all. Everyone knew exactly where they were supposed to be, and what they were supposed to be doing, at any given moment. Backstage was quiet and super-organized.

Elizabeth let us peek through the heavy curtain at the people filing in to take their seats, so we could answer the stage manager's question: "How's the house tonight?" The house was full, and *The Body in the Garage* started at eight o'clock sharp.

Elizabeth told us the Sturgis Theater hadn't put its stage lighting on a computer yet. She'd be busy at the big controlboard at the back of the balcony, where she could see the whole stage. She wore a headset, and flipped the switches and adjusted the dimmers as the stage manager directed her. She didn't have time to be talking to us, so we watched the actors from the wings.

The Body in the Garage was a funny play, about a mechanic who thinks he sees a murder, drives the police crazy trying to convince them that there has been a murder when there's no body, and eventually finds the body sitting in the backseat of the car he's been working on. But it was Act 2, Scene 1, that Patti and Kate and I found most exciting: Vernon, the murderer, was arguing with his ex-girlfriend. Her name was Marsha, but otherwise it all sounded very familiar.

"Marsha, I'm telling you . . ." Vernon said, ". . . just keep away from me."

"A big strong man like you, afraid of little old me?" Marsha replied.

Vernon spoke again. "Marsha, don't come any closer. . . ."

Marsha kept walking toward him.

"I'm warning you . . ." Vernon said.

"You don't have the guts!" Marsha sneered.

Vernon reached into his coat pocket, and Marsha started wrestling with him. There was a loud bang . . . and the stage went dark!

"Did you hear that?" Patti whispered.

"It's just like the tape," murmured Kate, "only we could hear both parts."

We couldn't bother Elizabeth with it in the middle of Act 2. We had to wait until the whole play was over at the end of Act 3, and the curtain had come down, and the actors had taken their bows with spotlights on them. When Elizabeth finally switched off the board, took off her headphones, and came backstage, we rushed to tell her about my missing suitcase, and the tape, and the conversation at the end of it.

"What was the name on the reel?" Elizabeth asked.

"C. Harkness," I replied.

Elizabeth grinned. "Small world," she said. "C. Harkness is Charlie Harkness, the man who wrote this play. Sometimes he reads his scripts into a tape recorder while he's working on them, to see how they sound."

"Oh, wow!" Maybe I *was* going to get my clothes back! "Do you know how to get in touch with him?"

"He has a cabin somewhere upstate, with no phone," Elizabeth answered. "He has lots of friends in the city. It's really impossible to say where he might be staying. But he drops by here sometimes. As soon as he does, I'll ask him to call you in Riverhurst. I imagine he'd like his hiking boots back, too."

After we left the theater, we went to Elizabeth's apartment to say good-bye to Max. He'd been to the veterinarian's, and he looked like a different dog! After a bath, he was light brown, with curly hair, and he was wearing a brand-new blue collar. There was a bandage on his left hind leg, but otherwise he was fine. "The doctor said it was a bad sprain," Elizabeth told us. We all pigged out on brownies and hot apple cider, and then Elizabeth took us to Mrs. Bricker's.

"Stephanie's gone to bed. Did you have a good time?" she asked us as we took off our jackets and flopped down in the living room.

"Great! Mrs. Bricker, we found out who C. Harkness is — " I began.

"Charles Harkness, the playwright," Mrs. Bricker said with a smile. "I remembered right after you left. I read an article about *The Body in the Garage* a few weeks ago; it told how he uses a tape recorder in his work."

"Did Stephanie have a good time with Tiffany, Mrs. Bricker?" Patti asked.

"I'm afraid not." Mrs. Bricker shook her head disapprovingly. "Tiffany Parks had something better to do — she stood us up."

Chapter
11

Stephanie told us about it the next morning. "Tiffany finally called from a friend's house at about eight-thirty," Stephanie said. "She'd forgotten all about going skating with me!"

Stephanie faced Kate then. "You were right, Kate. I always thought Tiffany was somebody special, that anything she did was fine because she was so talented. But it's not fine — she's a crummy friend."

I was sorry Stephanie had to find out the hard way about Tiffany. Myra Dillard is living proof that you don't have to be stuck-up to be a star. She acts just like a regular person, only she has this great voice and plays electric keyboard almost as well as Spud Zircon, who's the new keyboard player for my favorite new rock group, Boodles.

Patti called Myra after breakfast that Sunday. Myra has her own answering machine, and she'd taped a message just for us: "Patti, Kate, Lauren, and Stephanie, this is Myra. I'm out for a second, picking up some stuff to eat, but I'll definitely be back before eleven — see you then? 'Bye."

Stephanie didn't want to go at first. She was feeling pretty down. But Patti said, "Please don't let Tiffany ruin your whole weekend."

"Besides, can you think of anything that would bug Tiffany Parks more than hearing you were visiting Myra?" Kate pointed out.

Stephanie managed to pull herself together. First we packed — easy for me, since I didn't have anything to put in a suitcase except Mr. Harkness's hiking clothes — so we'd be ready to leave for Riverhurst that afternoon. Then we went downstairs to the lobby, where Will, the day doorman, got us a cab.

Stephanie perked up on the way over to Myra's. We passed the place where we'd found Max — the car I'd crawled under was still parked by the curb — and the bus stop where the bus and Patti had left without us. Then we passed the Lucretia Mott School, where both Stephanie and Patti once went.

Myra's family lives in the first two floors of a townhouse. She was waiting for us on the front stoop. "Hi! I'm glad all of you came, because my mom and I bought a ton of food!" she said, leading us through a carved wooden door at the top of the steps. Inside, we met Myra's parents, her baby sister Suzanne, and her older brother. Then we followed her to the back of the house. "This is where we practice," Myra told us.

"Practice what?" Stephanie asked.

Myra pushed open the door to a large, sunny room with windows that looked out on a tiny garden. In the middle was a shiny black grand piano. At one end stood an electric keyboard, some drums, and a big tape deck, and at the other end was a video camera on a stand.

"Wow! Who uses all this stuff?" Kate rushed over to check out the video camera.

"My dad and I both play the piano," Myra replied. "Tommy plays the drums, and Mom videotapes us. The electric keyboard is mine — I sing and play in a group sometimes."

"We heard," I said.

"You did?" Myra looked surprised. "From whom?"

"Tiffany Parks," Kate answered, glancing at Stephanie.

"Oh — Tiffany." Myra nodded. "She wanted to be in Breakout — that's the band — herself."

"What happened?" Stephanie asked.

Myra shrugged her shoulders. "Tiffany can't sing. She was furious when the group turned her down, but she just can't carry a tune."

"Really?" Stephanie asked. I think she was beginning to realize that maybe Tiffany Parks was not nearly so talented as she said she was.

But Myra was great! She played and sang a couple of songs for us, including part of a tune she actually was writing along with a guy from her band. Then we all dug into a pile of ham and cheese croissants and a bowl of macaroni salad. We had lime ice cream and little blueberry tarts for dessert. Just listing the food we ate during the weekend was going to take up two or three pages of my journal — *if* I ever saw my journal again.

Kate got to use the video camera, Tommy gave a short performance on the drums, and Myra promised to visit us in Riverhurst. Then it was time to get back to Mrs. Bricker's to pick up our stuff.

I think of that weekend in the city as the "lost and found" weekend. Stephanie lost her friend Tiffany Parks, but we found new friends in Elizabeth and Max, and Myra Dillard.

Max was lost and found, Patti found she could manage in the city just fine, and Kate found some things about the city she actually liked — mimes and hailing a cab, for instance.

I lost my suitcase and my favorite sweater, but got them back, sooner than I thought I would, too.

I was at the board on Monday, working on a

math problem, when the intercom announced: "Lauren Hunter, please come to the principal's office."

Patti and Kate and Stephanie all stared at me. When had I had time to get into trouble?

"Go ahead, Lauren," Mrs. Mead said. "Sally, please come up and finish the problem."

I hurried down the hall to Mrs. Wainwright's office, feeling a little queasy, the way you do when you have to see the principal.

"Go right in," the secretary told me. "Mrs. Wainwright's on the telephone."

Mrs. Wainwright waved me into a chair and took the phone away from her ear. "Lauren, did you lose a suitcase in the city on Friday?"

I nodded.

"There's a gentleman on the telephone who says he'll put your suitcase on the four o'clock bus from the city. And he'd like you to put his suitcase on the five o'clock from Riverhurst *to* the city."

C. Harkness! How did he find me? Well, it turned out that he saw "Riverhurst" and "Lauren" on the cover of my journal, then looked inside and read "Patti," and "Kate," and "Stephanie." Then he called the school and asked if they could help. They said yes, of course: *Everybody* knows the Sleepover Friends!

#6 Kate's Camp-Out

Dr. Beekman had been upstairs, exploring the second floor of the house. "I know how you girls like your privacy, so you can have the whole floor to yourselves — I lit a kerosene lantern for you."

That would have been great news any other time, but *that* night, in *that* house, I was thinking about safety in numbers. Patti and Stephanie and I stared uneasily at the steep stairs leading to the second floor and then at Kate.

"We're not sleepy yet, Dad," Kate said. "Why don't we sit around, finish the fudge, talk for a while? You can tell us about this place."

"Yes, Dr. Beekman, like why it's called Spirit Lake," said Stephanie.

Dr. Beekman sat down on the mouse-eaten couch. The rest of us were leaning against the luggage, Patti and Stephanie had pulled their sleeping bags up around their shoulders.

"Well, there are several stories about that," Dr. Beekman began. "And one of them is a little spooky."

Spooky? A chill ran down my spine. . . .